Funny Bunny

by Sally Doherty

illustrations by
Dubravka
Kolanovic

It was a beautiful day.

Mother Bunny and
Franny Bunny decided
to go to the park.

"Look at me!"
said Franny.

"Oh you're my
funny bunny,"
said Mother Bunny.

Then they had
lunch under a tree.

"Look at me!"
said Franny.

"Oh you're my
funny bunny,"
said Mother Bunny.

After lunch
it was naptime.

Mother Bunny and
Franny went home.

Before Franny curled up to sleep, she said, "Look at me!"

"Oh you're my funny bunny," said Mother Bunny.

After Franny's
nap it began
to rain.

Franny
played inside.

"Look at me!" said Franny, but before Mother Bunny could stop her, CRASH! "Oh no!"

Franny was sorry.